13th STREET

Fight with the Freeze-Ray Fowls

Read more 13th Street books!

HARPER **Chapters**

13th STREET

Fight with the Freeze-Ray Fowls

by DAVID BOWLES

illustrated by SHANE CLESTER

HARPER

An Imprint of HarperCollins*Publishers*

To John Picacio and the rest of my hermanes
in the Mexicanx Initiative. X-up!

13th Street #6: Fight with the Freeze-Ray Fowls
www.harperchapters.com
Library of Congress Control Number: 2021936550
ISBN 978-0-06-300963-9 — ISBN 978-0-06-300962-2 (pbk.)
Typography by Torberg Davern and Catherine Lee
21 22 23 24 25   PC/LSCC   10 9 8 7 6 5 4 3 2 1

First Edition

CONTENTS

CHAPTER 1

BENEATH THE BRIDGE

Ivan hated being late, even for a dangerous mission to a spooky dimension.

"Hurry up, Aunt Lucy!" he called.

Ivan was standing on the steps to Lucy's apartment building with his cousins, Malia and Dante. Tapping her foot beside them was their friend Susana Leal. She'd come with them to Gulf City to enjoy the New Year's Eve fireworks display over Karankawa Bay.

Of course, neither Mr. Leal nor Aunt Lucy knew the real reason the four kids had begged permission to come.

They were going to return to 13th Street.

Dozens of children from across Texas had wandered into that scary place, and now they were the captives of a wicked queen. Someone had to set them free!

"Coming!" shouted Lucy. She popped through the door and pulled a flowery shawl

over her head. "Oooh, it's chilly. Y'all have your jackets?"

"Yup!" said Malia, zipping hers up. "Christmas present from my mom. **VERY** expensive."

Ivan rolled his eyes and pulled on the straps of his backpack.

"Why do you kids always carry those everywhere?" Lucy asked.

"It's a wild world," Dante explained.

"Gotta be ready for anything. Tidal waves, shark attacks, the zombie apocalypse . . ."

Lucy pinched his cheek, laughing. "Like any of those things could ever happen to y'all. Come on, pingos!" she said, teasing.

They hurried to the bus stop. In a matter of minutes, they were standing on the shore. They found a good spot close to the bridge that stretched across Karankawa Bay, joining Gulf City to Invader Island.

Ivan glanced around, looking for the Aguilars. Suddenly, out of the crowd came Mickey and Doña Chabela.

"Hey, guys!" Mickey said, holding out his fist. Ivan and Dante bumped it with theirs. Malia gave him a salute and a smile.

"Are your parents here?" Lucy asked.

Chabela pointed up the beach. "They've set up chairs under that purple umbrella. Mickey and I were just going to get elotes. Want to come, kids?"

Everyone looked over at the food cart selling corn on the cob.

"Y'all go with Mickey," Lucy suggested, "and I'll say hi to Mickey's parents. Will you introduce me, Doña Chabela?"

"Of course," the old lady said. Then she turned to her grandson, whispering, "Good luck."

As the two women walked away, the kids walked toward the food cart.

"Whew," groaned Ivan. "Cutting it close! Mickey, did you hack in?"

Mickey arched an eyebrow. "Oh, yeah. I made a shortcut to the Lake. I can open the portal with this."

He waved his smartphone in the air.

Susana sighed. "Good. Let's go over the plan again."

Dante rolled his eyes. "Our plans never work. We should just trust our gut."

"No." Ivan shook his head. He was not a fan of the unexpected. "We might have to think on our feet, but we need to know our plan inside and out."

Mickey nodded. "Agreed. So, we arrive at the lakeshore, then we take the ferry to the island. I have friends in the Red Tower. They'll sneak us in while the chaneks attack and keep Her Noisy Majesty busy. We'll find the kids and bring them back."

The group passed the elote cart and hurried to the bridge. Mickey tapped his phone, and a faint purple glow came from beside a concrete column.

One by one, the others passed through the portal until just Ivan stood on the sand. Ivan tried not to think about all the things that could go wrong. Taking a deep breath, he entered 13th Street for what he hoped was the last time.

CHAPTER

2

THE END OF THE STREET

Ivan emerged on another shore, covered with pebbles instead of sand. Before him spread a lake that disappeared into strange gray mists on either side. In the middle of the lake was an island, where a tower of red stone rose. Moving slowly between the shore and the lake was a flat boat.

WHOOSH!

Ivan turned to see the portal disappear as Mickey put his phone away. Behind him stretched a gravel road with abandoned mansions along either side.

The last block of 13th Street.

"Talk about dead ends," Dante announced. "This is the deadest of all."

"Where your dad jokes come to die," Susana muttered.

"This is where you arrived the first time

you came to 13th Street, right?" Malia said to Mickey.

Mickey nodded. "Yes. Captain Kamak found me and took me to the queen."

"You never told us how you became the Quiet Prince," Malia said.

"It's a little embarrassing. The queen decided to, uh, adopt me." Mickey blushed. "I just wanted to find Bruno, but she wouldn't let me leave the island.

I was trapped in the Red Tower for a year. But I was nice to her and earned her trust. When she named me prince and put the knights under my command, I used them to escape."

"Ah," Ivan said. The rest he pretty much knew. Mickey had given his knights their next command—to find Bruno—and then lost control of them. He'd spent the next few years in hiding, trying to help the residents of 13th Street fight back against the queen.

As if on cue, a group of creepy creatures appeared. Ivan could make out a few calacas, a pair of ghosts, a pack of werewolves, a dozen disembodied hands skittering along like spiders, and a giant.

Susana gasped in horror.

Malia clenched her fists. "Get your guard up, guys," she grunted.

Dante muttered, "Uy, cucuy."

"Perfect timing!" Mickey grinned. "A new batch of passengers. We'll get across on the ferry with them. Come on!"

The boat Ivan had seen earlier was pulling up to a dock. The creatures made their way to it. The person piloting the boat let them on board one by one.

As the kids ran toward the dock, Ivan saw that the pilot was a **MUMMY**!

"That's one way to not get sunburned," Dante laughed. "Wrap yourself in bandages!"

Susana elbowed him. "There's no sun, doofus. It's the Underworld."

Dante pointed up. "What do you call that orange circle? A floating tangerine?"

"It's an illusion," Mickey said, heading toward the boat.

They hurried down the dock as the giant got onto the ferry. The mummy pilot looked at them and lifted a bandaged hand.

"No. Sorry, Your Silent Highness," it said in a raspy voice.

"Captain Kimrir!" Mickey said, his voice full of authority. "I command you to let us on board."

"I can't take living children to the island, Lord Micqui. Not without cocoons or spider guards." Kimrir the mummy pointed at the Red Tower. "The queen would unwind me for sure!"

3

BRUNO'S BIG BACK

"What now?" Ivan asked. The plan was already falling apart. He felt nervous. Sure, when things had gone wrong in the past, they'd managed to think fast and avoid danger. But there was a lot more pressure now, with so many kids trapped in 13th Street and no one to help them.

"Should we swim?" Dante asked.

Mickey shook his head. "Living people have to be ferried across. Nothing else works. Not even my cape. It lets me teleport anywhere I want. But not here. That's why I was with the chaneks in the skull ship when you found me in the sewer. The idea was to sail to the last block and cross the Lake to rescue the kids."

"Oops," Susana said, raising an eyebrow. "I guess the Tremendous Trio here ruined that plan, huh?"

"Dude," Dante replied. "We were trying to reunite Mickey with Bruno

and bring him back to his parents."

Ivan snapped his fingers excitedly. An idea

had popped into his head, something he'd read in one of the books in their school library.

"Bruno," he said. "Perfect! The Aztecs believed that people crossed over water into the Underworld on the backs of dogs."

Mickey's eyes widened. "Dante, do you still have his squeaky toy?"

Dante unzipped the front pocket of his backpack and pulled out the rubber rabbit. "Want me to call him?"

"No," Malia said, "we want you to throw it into the water. **YES, OF COURSE**, doofus. Squeeze it!"

SQUEEEEAAAAK!
WHOOOOSH!

Standing before them, surrounded by a glow, was the Irish wolfhound!

"Good boy!" Mickey said, hugging Bruno's neck. "Can you take us to that island?"

Bruno answered with a bark.

Susana narrowed her eyes. "Um, guys? He's big, but the five of us aren't going to fit on his back."

As if to answer her, Bruno started shaking himself. To their surprise, **HE GOT BIGGER AND BIGGER**! Pretty soon, he was the size of a small boat! He waded into the water and turned to bark at them again.

Malia laughed and nudged Susana. "You were saying? Come on, y'all!"

CHAPTER

4

FREEZE-RAY FOWLS!

As Bruno dog-paddled his way across the lake, Ivan smiled to himself. This was how you handled the unexpected. Not trusting your gut, like Dante said. No, you studied hard and memorized information. Then you used that knowledge to figure out a solution.

About halfway across the lake, Mickey held his hands to his mouth and called, "Come, ko-HEN!"

Dante tapped his shoulder. "Are you sending a signal to your friends?"

"Yes. To a brave owl named Tunk. He taught me how to fool the queen," Mickey explained.

Bruno reached the island shore, and the children got off his back. The dog stood in the shallows, whining.

"Dogs aren't allowed on the island," Mickey said. "Their job is to bring souls across. That's as far as the queen lets them come."

"Ah," said Dante, nodding. "A cat person, huh?"

There was a sound, like wings flapping. Ivan looked up at the Red Tower. A large bird came flying down from one of the windows, spiraling through the air. It was a screech owl, Ivan realized.

"Whoa," Malia muttered. "It's almost as big as you, Dante."

Susana laughed. "Which isn't saying much."

"Tunk! Old friend!" Mickey called, waving at the owl as it landed near them.

"It is good to see you, Lord Micqui," Tunk answered, his voice deep. "Though it was unwise to return."

"I had to. For the children," Mickey replied. "Can you get us inside?"

Tunk closed his eyes and lowered his head as if in shame. "Yes."

SQUAAAAAWK!
SCREEEECH!

A massive flock of owls, vultures, and turkeys burst from the windows of the tower! They swooped toward the cousins!

BLUE RAYS OF LIGHT SHOT FROM THEIR EYES!

Ivan's heart started pounding. Tunk had betrayed Mickey!

"**RUN!**" shouted Susana, heading back toward Bruno.

As the others started to follow, the fowls kept shooting blue beams. One hit Susana, turning her blue! She instantly froze in place and fell over onto the sand.

Bruno barked and howled in the water, but there was nothing the dog could do.

"**FREEZE RAYS!**" Ivan managed to yell. Then a cold sensation slammed into his back and he couldn't move anymore.

Four chapters down! That's pretty cool—but not freezing!

CHAPTER

5

ROYAL REVELATIONS

Once all five children were frozen, the freeze-ray fowls grabbed them and flew into the Red Tower. Even though he couldn't move, Ivan could still see. As they twisted and turned through hallways, he looked carefully at every detail. He needed to find a connection to what he'd studied in that library book. It was the only way out of this situation.

Finally the birds came to a huge chamber with a high ceiling. Along the walls stood guards: Aztec mummies with swords and cackling cougars with spears.

On a raised throne sat the queen, wearing a gown covered with bones. Titan tarantulas crouched on either side of her.

A huge white barn owl landed on the back of the throne. It cawed, "All hail Her Noisy

Majesty, the Loud Lady, our glorious Queen of Bones!"

The freeze-ray fowls dropped the children before her. They were still frozen in scared poses, which made the queen double over with laughter.

"Oh, yes!" she shouted. Ivan would have winced at the sound, but he couldn't move a muscle. "My rebellious heir and his annoying little friends. I knew this day would come! Your minds will make lovely additions to my collection."

Ivan had no idea what she was talking about. He found it hard to think. It was like his brain had filled up with fear and stress. No matter how hard he tried, he couldn't remember a single helpful fact.

"But you don't understand, do you? The Quiet Prince only told you what he wanted you to know. Let me explain what's really going on."

Ivan was glad he couldn't move, because he would have laughed out loud. She was going to tell them her plan, just like a villain in some silly movie.

"I should thank Micqui, to be

honest." The queen petted the tarantula to her right. "I was so tired of being second best, of bowing to my sister, Lady Blood. But I can whisper into the minds of grieving humans. I kept searching for one with the right amount of imagination and skill. When I found him, he was sad about his stupid dog. So all it took was a few dreams. Before I knew it, he had created a realm for me. Then he sealed it off from my sister's control! And for a year, I kept him by my side. I found I could use his creative mind to rule 13th Street. I was a queen at last."

Ivan was shocked. Mickey had lied, telling them that 13th Street was his idea. He'd never mentioned the Loud Queen's role.

"Oh, but then the brat ran off with my cougars," the queen continued. "And 13th Street started to crumble."

Ah! Ivan thought. That explained the tilting buildings, the hot warehouses, and the glitching spots they'd seen.

"I knew that before long, Lady Blood

would break through the gates," the queen added. "I needed more children like Micqui! I found his grandmother and made her send you three cousins. But you escaped!"

That much Ivan already knew, from Chabela herself.

"So," the queen said, leaning forward on her throne, "I opened all the portals and let foolish kids wander right into my grasp. Their terrified imaginations have kept 13th Street scary and under my control!"

The queen stood, bony wings spreading from her back as she raised her voice to a spooky cry:

"Now, meddling children, your minds will join theirs!"

CHAPTER

6

ATOP THE RED TOWER

The Queen of Bones gave a cruel smile. "Time for a little marching. Guards, get a gag ready. The prince knows too many spells. Here we go. Unfreeze, chah-BAR!"

The cold suddenly left Ivan, and he dropped to his knees, gasping.

Dante did the same right beside him. But his cousin was giggling. "Dude, she monologued!"

Ivan tried to smile at his cousin's big word. "Yup. Spilled her entire plan."

Dante shrugged. "I guess villains gonna villain."

Aztec mummies had gagged Mickey. Cackling cougars were nudging Susana and Malia to their feet with spears.

Tunk and another screech owl flew over to Dante and Ivan, yanking them to their feet with sharp talons.

"Move!" Tunk snarled.

Shaking with laughter, the Queen of Bones crooked a finger at the children. "Come, girls and boys. Walk this way."

Head held high, the noisy monarch strode toward an archway.

"Does she mean walk like a stuck-up evil weirdo,"

Susana muttered, "or do we follow her?"

The cougar behind her laughed. "Good one! But, yeah, move it."

Tunk and the guards marched the kids up a spiraling staircase. Ahead of them, the Queen of Bones was whistling away, apparently in a really good mood.

The walk was long and it gave Ivan time to think. Not about his library book, but about his first adventure in this world. He remembered being attacked by the Snatch Bats and jumping from rooftop to rooftop.

He had known nothing about 13th Street, but he had learned on the fly.

Maybe that's all he needed to do now.

As they reached the very top of the stairs, Tunk shoved Ivan with his claws. Getting his beak close to Ivan's ear, Tunk muttered, "I'm still on your side. Get ready to fly."

Ivan's eyes went wide. Tunk was a double agent! He'd been pretending to betray them the whole time!

The queen opened a door, and everyone emerged onto the roof of the tower.

Ivan drew a sharp breath, startled. Chairs were arranged in a circle all around the edge. Sitting in most of them were dozens of children with their eyes closed.

Metal caps were strapped to their heads, and hazy beams of energy flowed from them straight into the gray sky above.

CHAPTER

7

AVIAN ALLIES

"Oh, look at the tears in your eyes," the queen said mockingly. "Boo-hoo! Don't worry. They don't feel a thing. They're just dreaming. Forever."

"Shall we find them a seat?" Tunk asked.

The queen nodded. "Yes. Let's make them comfortable. With their clever imaginations, I can expand 13th Street even farther!"

As Tunk guided him toward an empty seat, Ivan glanced over the low wall. Below, on the other side of the tower, a bridge stretched out over the lake. On the far shore, there was just a swirling gray mist and a huge black gate, locked with chains and guarded by Snatch Bats.

One of the cackling cougars pushed Susana down onto a chair. Another was about to do the same to Malia when . . .

WHOOP WHOOP WHOOSH!

A half dozen screech owls came flying up from below, shooting freeze rays at the mummies and cougars!

PEW! PEW! ZAP! ZAP!

"Traitors!" screamed the queen.

Tunk grabbed Ivan around the waist and launched into the air. "Hold on!" he cried.

Two more owls took Mickey by the arms and flew off with him, too.

"Oh, no, you don't!" shouted the queen. "Fall down, cham-SAR!"

ERRRR THUD!

Mickey and his rescuers dropped from the sky, landing on the roof.

The queen yanked Dante up and shoved him into the empty chair next to Susana. "You're not going anywhere."

She whirled around to find Malia.

"You're next!" the queen cackled.

"Wrong!" she shouted.

Ivan gasped as Malia ran toward the edge of the roof and jumped.

8

SIGNAL FROM THE SKY

Ivan couldn't understand how his cousin could take such a chance. It was a literal leap of faith!

But sure enough: one of Tunk's fellow owls caught Malia on its back, beating the air with its wings and lifting her to safety.

For now, at least.

On the rooftop, the queen turned to Susana and Dante. Smiling cruelly, she strapped the bronze caps onto the children's heads.

"No!" shouted Ivan.

"Let them go!" screamed Malia.

Ivan couldn't hear the words the queen whispered into their ears, but Dante and Susana closed their eyes at once.

And bright beams shot from their heads into the gray sky above.

Their imaginations, Ivan realized. She was draining their dreams.

"Come on, icy eyes!" Malia demanded. "Zap her!"

"We can't," her rescuer said. "Our freeze rays do not work on the queen."

"We have to help," Ivan pleaded with Tunk. "Please."

"The only way to save them is by carrying out the Quiet Prince's plan," the owl replied. "His chanek allies attack and you

rescue the children while she's distracted."

The Queen of Bones turned to Mickey, who lay at her feet. The fall had knocked him out.

"Malia!" Ivan called to his cousin. "How

was Mickey going to signal the chaneks?"

Anger drained from her face, replaced by hope.

Closing her eyes, Malia shouted with all the strength she had:

"Protect us, Shi-YA-na!"

CHAPTER

9

THE FOWLS FOLLOW!

"Attack!" screamed the queen.

A black cloud of predator birds burst from the Red Tower. Tunk and his half dozen allies turned tail and flew as fast as they could, carrying Ivan and Malia toward the bridge.

Would the chaneks get here soon enough?

Cold blue beams streaked through the air around them. Tunk did a barrel roll to avoid getting hit. Ivan's stomach flopped. He almost threw up the cheese enchiladas Aunt Lucy had fed them for lunch.

Close by, Malia's owl was also diving and spinning.

"Ahhh!" shouted Malia. "I really don't like this!"

"Listen, Ivan," Tunk said to him. "We can't cross the water. The queen doesn't trust us.

But if you and Malia can open that gate, she will lose her power. Thirteenth Street will be no more."

"I don't understand," Ivan said.

"There are four roads into the Underworld," the owl explained.

Ivan remembered this from his research. "Oh! Black, white, red, and green."

"Exactly," Tunk said. "And 13th Street is the Black Road, Ivan. The queen used Micqui to seal it off. She transformed it with his imagination and shut it away."

In a flash, Ivan understood. "On the other side of that gate is the rest of the Underworld!"

"And so is its true leader, Lady Blood, older sister of that noisy creature back there," Tunk added. "If you open the gate for her, she will end this illusion at last and free all the children."

¡Vas volando! You're flying through this book!

CHAPTER

10

BINOCULARS ON THE BRIDGE

After a few more seconds of dodging freeze rays, the good owls set Ivan and Malia down on the bridge. Then they flew back up and returned to battle. Ivan told Malia what Tunk had said to him about the gate.

"Have you seen all the bad-breath bats flying around it?" Malia asked.

"The queen's sister is on the other side," Ivan explained. "Tunk swears if we open the gate, she'll fix everything."

"Then let's go for it!" Malia said.

They ran up the bridge, stopping once they were above the water. Malia turned and looked back at the Red Tower. Blue lightning was crackling all around its top.

"Oh no! What's happening to Dante and Susana? Is Mickey okay?" Malia cried.

Ivan yanked his backpack off his back and started rummaging around. He pulled out a pair of binoculars and focused on the tower.

"The queen is using her dark-side lightning powers to lift Mickey into the air," he said, trying not to be scared.

Malia's face went pale. "What about the others?"

"They're just sitting there, asleep. Wait!" Ivan fiddled with the focus knob. "Dante just opened his eyes a little! He's . . . he's . . . reaching out to Susana! He just grabbed her hand!"

Malia seemed confused. "Wait, what?"

"Susana opened her eyes, too! And now . . .

wow!" Ivan couldn't believe what he was seeing. "Their imagination streams . . . are combining!"

"Those two weirdos have the biggest imaginations I know," Malia said. "That dumb queen doesn't know what she's gotten herself into!"

Ivan pumped his fist in the air. "Yes! Their stream is bending toward the queen! She has no idea what's happening!"

Then he began to scan the lake and something else came into view. "Malia! It's the skull ship. The chaneks are coming!"

11

CHANEKS AND A CHOICE

Ivan watched through the binoculars as the Queen of Bones shrieked in anger. The chaneks got off their ship and started flinging vines. As the little green elves climbed up the tower and over the stone wall, she looked right at Ivan.

"Guards!" she shouted. "To the bridge!"

A flood of cougars came rushing out of the tower.

"What are we waiting for?" Malia pulled off her backpack and took out her water gun. It was full of mouthwash.

Ivan rubbed a hand over his face. "What if it's a trick? Maybe Tunk's lying. Or maybe Lady Blood is bad, too."

Malia put her hand on his shoulder. "You're thinking too much, primo."

"But if I can't think, how can I make sure this will work?" Ivan asked.

Malia smiled. "Nothing is certain. Not in Nopalitos, or here on 13th Street. But we have each other's backs, Ivan. That's what matters."

Ivan grinned. His cousin was right.

"Now get out your water gun, and come shrink some stinky bats with me!" Malia said.

CHAPTER
12

THE BLACK GATE

"Let's do this," Ivan said. He took out his own water gun, and the two cousins ran toward the gate.

SCREEEECH!

Snatch Bats flew at them, but the kids squirted mouthwash with perfect aim.

THUD! THUD! THUD!

Bats hit the pebbly ground one after another, shriveling up and twitching.

But before Ivan and Malia could reach the gate, spears started whizzing past them! A group of cackling cougars and Aztec mummies had crossed the bridge and were closing fast.

"Go!" Malia shouted. "I'll hold them off!"

Instead of asking how, Ivan just kept running.

As he reached the gate, squirting the last couple of bats, he heard Malia shout, "Rise up, SHE-wa!"

Ivan turned and saw the cougars and mummies fly backward through the air and land in the lake. Beyond them, the chaneks had reached the top of the Red Tower. Raising his binoculars, Ivan saw them wrap a vine around Mickey, pulling him away from the Queen of Bones.

The fake queen saw Ivan at the Black

Gate and screamed in frustration. Flinging lightning from her fingers, she leaped from the tower and rode a blazing blue bolt right toward him.

Ivan turned toward the gate and lifted his hand. Behind him, the queen's roar of rage got louder! A strong wind started battering Ivan. Lightning flashed all around him.

Taking a deep breath, Ivan chanced one last glance over his shoulder.

Dante and Susana's imagination beam had bent completely! It was now pulsing through the air, heading straight for the queen!

Ivan closed his eyes, ignoring the wind and lightning. The trick wasn't going with his gut, he realized at last.

The trick was having faith in his family and friends. Believing in them. Trusting them.

I choose to believe, he thought deep in his heart. *If we stick together, everything will be okay.*

Alone in the middle of that chaos, Ivan Eisenberg whispered two words:

"Open, Hebaan."

CRAAAACK!

The chains shattered!

CREEEEAAAAK!

The gate swung open!

On the other side of it was a desert landscape. A black stone road stretched off into the distance. Standing on the road was a woman, black-eyed and dressed in red.

She looked at Ivan and smiled.

You made it past the gate! Almost done. Knew you could do it!

CHAPTER

13

FREEING FRIENDS

"Well done, Ivan." The Queen of the Underworld stepped through the gate and laid a gentle hand on his cheek.

She lifted her other hand.

"Enough," she said quietly.

The sounds of battle stopped. Ivan turned and saw birds landing, guards dropping their weapons, and chaneks kneeling in respect.

Then Ivan couldn't help but laugh.

The Queen of Bones had been pinned to the ground by Dante and Susana's imagination beam! As Ivan watched, she transformed into a beach ball, a ballerina, a bottle of bleach, and finally a bawling baby.

"Ah, little sister. That form suits you best." Lady Blood clapped her hands in delight. "Still, I must ask Dante and Susana to let you go."

The beam of imagination faded, and the sisters stood face-to-face. Lady Blood was like the noisy one's mirror twin, with brown skin and black braids instead of bone-white features and hair.

The true queen snapped her fingers, and her sister stood wrapped in chains.

"Off to the dungeon with you," Lady Blood said. "A few centuries locked away should help you reflect on the harm you have caused."

WHOOSH!

The Loud Queen disappeared without another peep.

Malia rushed over to Ivan and Lady Blood.

"Please, Your Highness," the girl begged. "Can you set our cousin and friends and all the other kids free?"

"Of course! And you can help me." The true queen snapped her fingers again, and

they were instantly transported to the top of the Red Tower. "Unstrap those beastly caps from their heads, will you?"

Ivan and Malia hurried from kid to kid.

When they were done, the queen said softly, "Awaken, dear children."

Susana and Dante were the first to jump from their chairs.

"Dude!" Dante shouted when he saw Ivan. "Did you see what we did?"

Ivan nodded, smiling. "Yup. It was pretty amazing. But, Dante? You're still holding Susana's hand."

Dante laughed. "Who cares? Come on, y'all! Group hug!"

Ivan's heart swelled with joy as his cousins and their friend squeezed each other tight.

Another set of arms wrapped around them. Ivan looked up.

It was Mickey, a tired grin stretched across his face.

CHAPTER

14

THE REAL ROAD RETURNS

The other children yawned and rubbed months of sleep from their eyes.

Ivan felt the Queen of the Underworld pull Mickey away.

"One last task," she said. "You must help me remove your illusion."

Ivan felt a strange sense of sadness. As spooky and weird as it had been, part of him would miss 13th Street.

Without it, he wouldn't have learned to have faith. Malia wouldn't have learned to believe in people and not things. Dante wouldn't have learned to let go of his vanity and his rivalry with Susana. And the friendship that now bound them all together wouldn't exist.

Lady Blood leaned her forehead against Mickey's. A strange glow surrounded them as the Quiet Prince closed his eyes.

WHOOSH!

Ivan felt a wave of energy rush through the gate. It rolled over the Red Tower and headed down the street.

As it passed, it transformed everything! Scary, run-down mansions became glittering temples and pyramids. The gravel and asphalt of 13th Street faded, revealing the dark flagstones of the Black Road.

"It's beautiful," Ivan whispered.

When their work was done, Lady Blood nodded at Mickey and the others.

"It is time I sent you home. Yet before I do so, a few of my subjects wish to bid you farewell."

WHOOSH!

Suddenly standing before the cousins on the rooftop were all their old allies: the ghost girl Yoliya, Omi from the Depot of the Dead, the zombie family, Peki the piko, and Alba the calaca.

Teary-eyed, the cousins hugged their friends and said their goodbyes.

"At least for now, muchachos," Omi said with a wink.

WHOOSH!

RUFF!

Bruno appeared before Mickey, putting his big ghost paws on his chest.

"You're such a good boy," Mickey said. "And I'll miss you forever. But now it's time to let you go. Take care of our friends, okay?"

Then the true queen gathered all the children around her, and with a final snap of her fingers, she sent them all home.

CHAPTER

15

FIREWORKS, FAMILY, FRIENDS

"Elotes," Ivan shouted, "quick! Before they notice anything!"

The cousins and their friends hurried back across the darkening beach to the corn on the cob vendor.

Snacks in hand, they rejoined their families just as the first rockets burst into flowery sparks above the water.

"Got what you wanted?" Chabela asked with a mischievous grin.

"Yes, ma'am," Ivan said, holding up his plain, buttered corn. "No more spooky surprises."

Dante chewed on his cob, which was covered with chili powder. "Don't worry, though. I'll still bring spice to everyone's life."

"¡Eso!" exclaimed Aunt Lucy. "Stay spicy."

Malia laughed. Her corn was dripping everything: mayo, cream, chili, butter. "Hey, life's too short not to enjoy the good stuff."

Susana turned to Mickey. "Tell me again why these weirdos are our friends?"

The older boy rubbed her head. "Simple. They're the bravest kids we know."

The children all leaned together, surrounded by family. They looked up in wonder as fireworks blossomed higher and higher, lighting the night sky brighter than the stars.

ACTIVITIES

THINK!

The cousins encounter a lot of birds—both good and bad! Think of a bird you've seen and draw it.

FEEL!

Ivan doesn't like surprises, but learns to have faith. How do you feel when you're surprised by something?

ACT!

Everyone eats elotes at the end! Find a video on how to make them and cook some with a grown-up.

DAVID BOWLES is the award-winning Mexican American author of many books for young readers. He's traveled all over Mexico studying creepy legends, exploring ancient ruins, and avoiding monsters (so far). He lives in Donna, Texas.

SHANE CLESTER has been a professional illustrator since 2005, working on comics, storyboards, commercials, and children's books. Shane lives in Florida with his two kids and his extensive action figure collection.